Alfie
Makes a Splash

Written and illustrated by
Keren Ludlow and Willy Smax

Orion
Children's Books

First published in Great Britain in 1996
by Orion Children's Books
a division of the Orion Publishing Group Ltd
Orion House
5 Upper St Martin's Lane
London WC2H 9EA

Based on a story from BENNY THE BREAKDOWN TRUCK
Text copyright © Willy Smax 1994, 1996
Illustration copyright © Keren Ludlow 1994, 1996

The right of Willy Smax and Keren Ludlow to be identified as the author and illustrator respectively of this work has been asserted.

A catalogue record for this book is available from the British Library
Printed in Italy
ISBN 1 85881 288 7

Mike McCannick walked into Smallbills Garage carrying a large can of 20/50 motor oil.

"Yum, yum," said Benny the Breakdown Truck. "My favourite."

"Sorry, Benny, but it's not for you," said Mike.

"I never get anything nice," grumbled Benny.

"That's because you're just a dusty old breakdown truck," said Francis Ford Popular.

"Expensive oil is for special cars like me."

"That's enough," said Mike. "Time for work, Benny. We've got to go and pick up some spare parts."

They drove off to the car spares shop.

"Oh-oh!" said Mike, looking in his rear-view mirror. "Look who's coming up behind."

It was Alfie Romeo the sports car, flashing his lights to overtake.

Mike and Benny watched as Alfie weaved through a gap in the traffic, nearly causing an accident.

"You're going too fast," said Benny as he pulled up behind Alfie at the traffic lights.

"Oh, shut up," said Alfie.

"I'm in a hurry. I'm going to take a short cut."

The lights changed and Alfie shot away again.

"Hey, don't go down there!" shouted Benny.

But Alfie didn't wait to listen.
He was going so fast that he

didn't see that his short cut
led straight down to the canal.

There was a huge SPLASH as
Alfie hit the water.

"Help! Help!" he shouted.
"I'm drowning!"

"Oh no!" said Mike. "Alfie's fallen in!"

Benny didn't waste any time.

He lowered his
big hook
over the
bridge
so that
it caught
Alfie's bumper.

Slowly he pulled the red sports car up, dripping with water.

Everyone cheered as Benny

proudly towed Alfie home.

Back at the garage, Mike dried out Alfie's engine and charged up his battery.

Soon Alfie was feeling fine.

"Thanks for pulling me out, Benny," said Alfie.

"That's okay," said Benny. "Just don't go speeding any more."

"No, I won't," said Alfie.

"Benny, you deserve a reward," said Mike.

He picked up the can of 20/50 motor oil and slowly poured it into Benny's engine.

"But that's only for
special cars like me,"
said Francis.

"Benny is special," said Mike.
"He saved Alfie's life."